D1369241

PRESENTED TO

_____

FROM

_____

Text copyright © 2003 by Melody Carlson

Illustration copyright © 2003 by Susan Reagan

Cover and interior design: Chris Gilbert - UDG | DesignWorks

Published in 2003 by Broadman & Holman Publishers,
Nashville, Tennessee

DEWEY: CE
SUBHD: NIGHT \ FEAR

ISBN 0-8054-2687-6

1 2 3 4 5   07 06 05 04 03

When the Creepy Things Come Out

Melody Carlson

Illustrations by Susan Reagan

Broadman & Holman Publishers   Nashville, Tennesee

I'm not scared of anything!

Nothing here is frightening.

Not flying bats,

Not big black cats.

I laugh at snakes,

That's all it takes.

Ha! Ha!

I'm as brave as I can be

No one dares sneak up on me...

What was that knock?

I'll bolt the lock!

A tiger and bear!

What a scare!

Oh, my!

I guess that I was wrong this time,

It's just my pals, Lee and Cline.

To visit me

And to see,

If I have something

Sweet to eat.

Come in!

Now it's getting dark outside,

And suddenly I want to hide.

A shrieking howl—

It's not an owl.

Wild wolves are out

Now hear me shout.

Help me!

Fiddlesticks, I should've known

Bowser only wants his bone

Or his dog food;

Or something good.

His tummy growled—

That's why he howled.

Here, boy!

On my way back to the house

I see something, it's not a mouse!

It's something hairy,

Something scary,

Running past

Very fast.

Yee-ikes!

So now I see it's a raccoon

Its coat is lit up by the moon.

But now I'm stuck,

And out of luck—

I can't get in!

Where's my brother Ben?

Open up!

I walk around to my front door...

But then I see them by the score!

Wild things prowling,

Monsters growling!

Some are green!

Some look mean!

Arrgh!!!!

Okay, so they looked real to me,

The neighbor kids, now I can see.

It's Anne and Tim,

And Josh and Jim.

Here for candy.

That's just dandy.

Oh, well.

At last it's time to go to bed.

Nothing here to fear or dread.

But it's still dark

Is that a shark?

I bet he'll eat

My hands and feet!

Yee-ow!!!

I laugh when I turn on the light.

My own shirt gave me such a fright.

Silly old me,

It's plain to see.

What a day—

It's time to pray!

Right now.

Dear God, I know that You are here,

I realize I don't need to fear.

For I can see

That You love me!

And this I know

I love You so!

Amen.

"Do not fear, for I am with you;

do not be dismayed, for I am your God.

I will strengthen you and help you;

I will uphold you with

my righteous right hand."

- I S A I A H 4 1 : 1 0